My Name Is Lucy

By Vanessa Julian-Ottie

GINGHAM DOG
P R E S S

Columbus, Ohio

For Graham, Lucy, and Holly

Children's Publishing

This edition published in the United States of America in 2003 by
Gingham Dog Press
an imprint of McGraw-Hill Children's Publishing,
a Division of The McGraw-Hill Companies
8787 Orion Place
Columbus, Ohio 43240-4027

www.MHkids.com

Printed in Singapore by Imago

0-7696-3007-3

1 2 3 4 5 6 7 8 9 10 MP 09 08 07 06 05 04 03

The McGraw-Hill Companies

My name is Lucy.

I live with some very nice people.
They are good at playing games,
but I always win.

I love going for walks,

gardening,

washing day,

slippers,

and my squishy blue ball.

But most of all I love food.

One day, I saw all kinds of
yummy desserts on the dining room table.

Suddenly, the cat from next door jumped in through the window. I heard a crash.

I helped myself to some whipped cream.
Everybody was mad at me.
I don't know why.

"Bad dog!" they said and
sent me to my basket.

I watched the people clear everything away.

They looked at the tablecloth.
Then they looked at the cat.
"Bad cat!" they said.

And suddenly everything was all right again.

Then some children arrrived, and I had
lots of yummy things to eat.

I love parties!